Franklin Plants a Tree

From an episode of the animated TV series *Franklin* produced by Nelvana Limited, Neurones France s.a.r.l. and Neurones Luxembourg S.A.

Based on the Franklin books by Paulette Bourgeois and Brenda Clark.

TV tie-in adaptation written by Sharon Jennings and illustrated by Sean Jeffrey, Mark Koren and Jelena Sisic.

Based on the TV episode *Franklin Plants a Tree*, written by Brian Lasenby.

Franklin

Franklin is a trademark of Kids Can Press Ltd.
The character Franklin was created by Paulette Bourgeois and Brenda Clark.
Text © 2001 Contextx Inc.
Illustrations © 2001 Brenda Clark Illustrator Inc.

Kids Can Press acknowledges the support of the Ontario Arts Council, the Canada Council for the Arts and the Government of Canada, through the BPIDP, for our publishing activity.

Published in Canada by
Kids Can Press Ltd.
29 Birch Avenue
Toronto, ON M4V 1E2

www.kidscanpress.com

Edited by Tara Walker

Printed in Hong Kong by Wing King Tong Company Limited

CM 01 0 9 8 7 6 5 4 3 2 1
CDN PA 01 0 9 8 7 6 5 4 3 2 1

Canadian Cataloguing in Publication Data

Jennings, Sharon
    Franklin plants a tree

(A Franklin TV storybook)
Based on characters created by Paulette Bourgeois and Brenda Clark.
ISBN 1-55074-878-5 (bound)   ISBN 1-55074-876-9 (pbk)

I. Bourgeois, Paulette. II. Clark, Brenda. III. Jeffrey, Sean. IV. Koren, Mark.
V. Sisic, Jelena. VI. Title. VII. Series: Franklin TV storybook.

PS8569.E563F778 2001   jC813'.54   C00-932221-3
PZ7.J46Fr 2001

Kids Can Press is a Nelvana company

Franklin Plants a Tree

Based on characters created by
Paulette Bourgeois and Brenda Clark

Kids Can Press

FRANKLIN could climb trees and swing from branches. He liked to play with his friends at the tree house and go for walks with his family in the woods. So Franklin was excited when he learned that Mr. Heron was giving away trees for Earth Day. He could hardly wait to have his own tree in his own backyard.

On Earth Day, Franklin got up early and dug a huge hole right outside his bedroom window. He wanted to plant his tree as soon as he got it home. Tonight, he'd invite his friends over to build a new tree house. Tomorrow, he'd look for an old tire and make a swing.

Franklin grabbed his wagon and hurried off. He didn't want all the big trees to be taken.

In the park, a large crowd was lined up in front of Mr. Heron. Franklin saw lots of boxes, but he didn't see the trees.

Maybe they're not here yet, he thought. Then he saw Rabbit leaving.

"Don't you want a tree?" Franklin asked.

"I have one," Rabbit replied, tapping his knapsack.

Franklin was confused.

Rabbit reached into his knapsack and pulled out a tiny tree.

"That's not a tree!" Franklin exclaimed. "That's a twig."

"It's a *baby* tree, Franklin," explained Beaver. "It's called a sapling. Mine's an ash and Rabbit has an oak."

"Well, I'm not getting a sapling," Franklin declared. "My tree has to be big enough to play in *today*."

But when Franklin got to the front of the line, Mr. Heron gave him a sapling the same size as the others.

"Could I have something bigger?" asked Franklin.

"This is a sugar maple," replied Mr. Heron. "Many years from now it will be very big indeed."

Franklin nodded sadly. He put the sapling in his wagon and walked slowly home.

Franklin sighed as he stared at the huge hole in his backyard. He shovelled earth back in until the hole was small. Then he went to get his sugar maple.

But the sapling wasn't there.

Franklin looked all around the garden and up and down the laneway.

It must have fallen out on the way home, he decided.

At lunchtime, Franklin told his parents about losing his tree.

"But it doesn't matter," he added. "It wasn't big enough to play in."

"Big or little, you promised to care for it," said his father.

Franklin slumped down in his chair.

"All right," he sighed. "I'll go look again."

Franklin followed the path back to the park.

By the pond, he saw Beaver. Her sapling was tied to a big stick marked with notches.

"It's a growth chart," Beaver explained. "In three years, my tree will be taller than me!"

Hmmm, thought Franklin. He began to look a little harder.

Near the woods, Franklin saw Bear painting a small fence bright red. Inside it was Bear's sapling.

"This will protect my pine tree until it's big and strong," Bear explained. "I don't want anyone to step on it by mistake."

Franklin thought about someone stepping on his sugar maple. If that happened, it would never grow big and strong and be taller than him.

Franklin told Bear everything.

"I've looked all over," Franklin moaned. "Now what do I do?"

"Maybe someone found your tree and gave it back to Mr. Heron," Bear suggested.

Franklin cheered up and ran off to find Mr. Heron.

Back at the park, Franklin saw Mr. Heron packing up boxes.

"How's your sapling doing in its new home?" Mr. Heron asked.

"I lost my tree, Mr. Heron," Franklin replied. "I've looked everywhere, but I can't find it."

Mr. Heron reached into a box and lifted
out a sapling.

"Is this it, Franklin?" he asked. "Someone
found it on the path."

"My tree!" cried Franklin. "Thank you,
Mr. Heron! I'm going to plant it right away."

Mr. Heron smiled.

Before Franklin left, Mr. Heron showed him a photograph.

"That's me when I was your age," he explained, "planting my first tree."

"Did it grow?" Franklin asked.

"It sure did," Mr. Heron laughed. "We're standing under it."

Franklin looked way, way up.

"You planted the tree house tree?!" he exclaimed. Then Franklin looked down at his sapling.

"Hmmm," he said thoughtfully.

Franklin hurried home, his sapling held safely in his arms. He planted it and watered it and then he checked on it every day. And, every day, Franklin was sure that his tree grew a little taller and a little stronger.

Just like Franklin.